RICHARD SCARRY'S
The Great Steamboat Mystery

When did Mrs. Pig's fabulous pearl necklace go missing? Crime-solvers Sam and Dudley search a steamship for the light-fingered jewel thieves.

RICHARD SCARRY'S

The Great Steamboat Mystery

STERLING CHILDREN'S BOOKS
New York

Mr. and Mrs. Pig just got married. They invited all their friends to a big wedding party aboard the steamboat *Sally*. Just for fun they asked everybody to wear a costume.

Mr. Pig also asked Sam and Dudley, the famous detectives, to come to the party. He wanted them to see that no wedding presents got stolen. Sam and Dudley wore costumes, too. They dressed like pirates.

"We must keep an eye on all the guests," said Pirate Sam. "A jewel thief is certain to sneak aboard in all this crowd."

When everyone was on board, the ship left the dock for a happy wedding party.

Sam and Dudley stopped to check with Mr. Pig.
"Shhh," said Mr. Pig. "Mrs. Pig is taking a nap in her deck chair. Just look at the beautiful pearl necklace she received as a wedding present."

Mr. Pig's favorite present was a gold pocket watch with an alarm.
He could set the alarm for any time and it would make a loud **B-R-R-I-N-N-G-G!**
when that time came around.

"You must be careful that your presents do not get stolen," said Sam,
as they went off to the dining room to see if everything was ready for the party.
They left Mrs. Pig snoozing all alone on deck.

While Mrs. Pig was sleeping, a pair of scissors suddenly appeared.

The scissors cut her string of pearls. Then two hands covered with white powder grabbed for the pearls as they slipped off the string. White powder flew all over Mrs. Pig's dress.

When she woke up she found, to her horror, that her pearls were missing. She ran into the dining room, screaming, "My pearls! My pearls! They have been stolen!"

"Whoever stole your pearls has gotten white powder all over your dress," said Sam. "The thief must have been covered with some sort of white powder. That clue should help us find the thief."

"Don't worry, Mrs. Pig," said Dudley. "We will find your pearls. Come, it's time to cut the cake."

The ship's baker brought in the wedding cake.
"Look!" said Dudley. "He is covered with white powder."
"It's white flour," said Sam. "We had better keep an eye on him."

The bride and groom cut the wedding cake.

All the guests sat down to eat a piece of the cake. Each piece had a prize baked into it. Mrs. Pig's prize was a pair of glass earrings.

"Hmm," whispered Sam. "The thief will try to smuggle Mrs. Pig's pearls ashore when the wedding party is over. We must watch what the baker takes with him. He might try to hide the pearls in another cake."

A little baby sat at one of the tables with his nursemaid.
He was feeding cake to his toy duck. "Isn't he cute?" said Dudley.
"Yes," said Sam. "But why is he covered with white powder?"
"Oh, he is such a little rascal," the nursemaid explained.
"He knocked over a can of talcum powder while I was changing
him this morning and he got it all over himself."

"Goo, goo," said the baby.
"Quack, quack," said the duck.

"Well, we must get to work," said Sam.
"Let's go out on deck. We might find some
white-powder clues there."

On deck they saw a suspicious-looking lady pirate.
She was covered with white powder and carrying a treasure chest.

"I'll bet Mrs. Pig's pearl necklace is hidden
in that chest," said Dudley. "Hurry! We must stop her
before she hides it somewhere."

Dudley came rushing around the corner just as the lady pirate was putting down her chest. He was going too fast to stop.

Ouch! His pirate sword rammed into her.
She screamed, leaped into the air . . .

. . . and over the side she went.
Dudley jumped right in after her.

"I will have the captain stop the boat," shouted Sam.

Dudley grabbed the lady pirate
and her treasure chest. Then Sam and
two sailors hauled them aboard.

The lady pirate was furious.
"You have ruined my sugar
doughnuts," she said. "Now they
are all wet."

"Sugar doughnuts! That is where
the white powder came from," thought Sam.
But he was still suspicious. She could be
hiding the pearls somewhere else.

As Sam and Dudley walked along the deck, they suddenly saw
white powder blowing through the slats of a door.

They tried to open the door. It was locked.
"Break down that door, Dudley!" shouted Sam.

Dudley smashed down the door. There sat a lady powdering her nose in front of a breezy porthole. She jumped up and tried to escape.

"STOP, THIEF!" shouted Dudley.

The lady stopped. She had to. She was stuck in the porthole. Sam and Dudley pulled and pulled . . .

. . . until the lady came unstuck.

"Why did you try to escape from us?" asked Sam.
"Well, wouldn't *you* try to escape if two pirates came
smashing through your door?" she answered.

"I didn't see any pearls on her," said Dudley as
they walked away.
"She *could* be the thief, though," said Sam. "She was
covered with white powder."
"Yes," Dudley agreed. "And that giant-size powder puff was
very suspicious. We had better keep an eye on her."

"Look!" said Sam. "Someone has left a trail of powder along
the deck. It may lead us to the thief."
"Stay out of our way, Little Rascal," said Dudley. "We are trying
to solve a mystery."

As they followed the trail, Dudley saw the baker in the kitchen,
baking another cake.
The lady pirate was sitting by her chest, eating soggy
sugar doughnuts.

Mrs. Pig was still crying over her lost pearls.

Mr. Pig was waiting for his watch to go B-R-R-I-N-N-G-G!

"We must find out where those pearls are hidden," said Sam. "But how do we go about it?"

"Aha!" cried Dudley. "The trail of powder is leaking from this keg. Maybe *this* is the big clue we need."

Boom!

Dudley and Sam suddenly flew into the air. One of the guests was using the white gunpowder to shoot his toy cannon.

"Well, that was certainly a *noisy* clue," said Dudley.
"Right," answered Sam. "And it gives me an idea. I think we should set a noisy *trap* to help us catch the thief."

They rushed back to Mr. Pig.
"I want to leave your watch where the thief can steal it,"
said Sam. "By using it for a trap, we will be able to find Mrs. Pig's
pearls when the thief tries to smuggle them off the ship."

Mr. Pig agreed, though he was afraid he might lose his watch, too.

Sam left the watch on deck—in plain view.
"Now let's get out of sight so the thief can steal it," he said.

Sure enough! When they returned a few minutes later, the watch was gone.
But there were white-powder marks on the deck—right where the watch had been.

"My trap worked," said Sam. "Now all we have to do is wait until people start to go ashore. We are coming into dock now."

As the guests gathered on deck, the ship's baker
appeared with a freshly baked cake.
"Aha!" said Dudley. "There is the thief and I know where
he has hidden the watch and necklace. Just watch me!"
He sliced furiously into the cake with his sword—
but there wasn't a thing hidden inside it!

The baker was furious. But since his cake was ruined
there was nothing to do but offer everyone a piece.

Little Rascal took a big piece of cake and walked away, pulling his duck behind him. As it rolled along, the duck started to lay tiny white eggs. "What a clever toy!" said Sam.

Suddenly—**B-R-R-I-I-N-N-G-G!**

A loud alarm went off.
The duck jumped. Everyone jumped.

"Those eggs! They're not eggs!" Sam shouted.
"They're pearls. And in a minute that duck is going
to lay a gold pocket watch! Don't let those thieves
get away!"

Little Rascal picked up his duck and
ran. His nursemaid followed him. They
crashed right into the lady pirate.

Everyone began to slip on the rolling pearls and before they knew it . . .

. . . overboard they all went!

SPLASH!

POP! SPLASH!

Little Rascal fell right into Sergeant Moriarty's lap.

"Arrest that baby!" Sam shouted. "He is a jewel thief."
"Why, bless my soul!" exclaimed Police Sergeant Moriarty. "It's not
a baby! It's Raffles Rat, the notorious jewel thief. And there is his
partner, Four-Finger Fox, hanging from our mast. I've been looking
all over for these thieves. I'm going to take them for a nice ride down
to the police station after I rescue those poor swimmers."

Dudley! Can't you get that duck to stop ringing?

BRINNNGG!

When everyone was safely back on board, they all started scrambling around to pick up the pearls and return them to Mrs. Pig.

She restrung them with thread and put them around her neck. She was happy once again.

Dudley made the duck lay a gold pocket watch so Mr. Pig was happy, too.

"How did you think of setting the trap with the watch?" Mr. Pig asked Sam.

"Well," said Sam, "I knew that the thief had to smuggle the pearls off the ship, but I didn't know where he would hide them. I decided that, if I could get him to steal the watch, he would have to hide that, too.

"But before I left the watch on deck, I set the alarm to go off at the time the boat would be landing. When I heard the alarm go off, I knew right away who the thief was."

"I must say," added Dudley, "that Little Rascal was very clever to dress up in baby clothes. Who would think that a baby could be a jewel thief?"

Mr. Pig thanked Sam and Dudley and paid them well for their clever detective work.

Mrs. Pig gave each of them a dozen big hugs and kisses to show her thanks.

As for Little Rascal and his partner, Sergeant Moriarty put them in jail, where they belonged.

STERLING CHILDREN'S BOOKS
New York

An Imprint of Sterling Publishing
387 Park Avenue South
New York, NY 10016

Published in 2014 by Sterling Publishing Company, Inc.
in association with JB Communications, Inc.
41 River Terrace, New York, New York
Previously published in 2008 by Sterling Publishing Company, Inc., in one volume with two other
Richard Scarry titles (*The Great Pie Robbery* and *The Supermarket Mystery*)
under the title *The Great Pie Robbery and Other Mysteries* (hardcover)

ISBN 978-1-4549-1010-7

Distributed in Canada by Sterling Publishing
c/o Canadian Manda Group, 165 Dufferin Street
Toronto, Ontario, Canada M6K 3H6
Distributed in the United Kingdom by GMC Distribution Services
Castle Place, 166 High Street, Lewes, East Sussex, England BN7 1XU
Distributed in Australia by Capricorn Link (Australia) Pty. Ltd.
P.O. Box 704, Windsor, NSW 2756, Australia

For information about custom editions, special sales, and premium and corporate purchases,
please contact Sterling Special Sales at 800-805-5489 or specialsales@sterlingpublishing.com.

Printed in China
Lot #:
2   4   6   8   10   9   7   5   3   1
11/13

www.sterlingpublishing.com/kids